I, *Geronimo Stilton*, have a lot of mouse friends, but none as spooky as my friend CREEPELLA VON CACKLEFUR! She is an enchanting and MYSTERIOUS mouse with a pet bat named **Bitewing**. Creepella lives in a CEMETERY, sleeps in a marble **sarcophagus**, and drives a **hearse**. By night she is a special effects and set designer for SCARY FILMS, and by day she's studying to become a journalist! Her father, Boris von Cacklefur, runs the funeral home Fabumouse Funerals, and the von Cacklefur family owns the CREEPY Cacklefur Castle, which sits on top of a skull-shaped mountain in MYSTERIOUS VALLEY.

YIKES! I'm a real 'fraidy mouse, but even I think Creepella and her family are AWFULLY fascinating. I can't wait for you to read this fa-mouse-ly funny and SPECTACULARLY SPOOKY tale!

Geronimo Stilton

Creepella von Cacklefur

Bitewing

Grandpa Frankenstein

Billy Squeakspeare

A journalist who lives in Mysterious Valley and solves spooky cases with her inseparable pet bat, Bitewing.

A famous writer and friend of Creepella.

An extremely mad scientist and an expert in Egyptian mummies.

Shivereen

Grandma Crypt

Snip and Snap

Troublemaking twins and expert spies.

Creepella's favorite niece.

Dolores

Kafka

The von Cacklefur family's pet cockroach.

She loves spiders, and her pet is a gigantic tarantula named Dolores.

Booey the Poltergeist

Boneham

Baby

He was adopted and raised with love by the von Cacklefurs.

The mischievous ghost who haunts Cacklefur Castle.

The butler to the von Cacklefur family, and a snob right down to the tips of his whiskers.

Chef Stewrat

Boris von Cacklefur

Madame LaTomb

The family housekeeper. A ferocious were-canary nests in her hair.

Chompers

The cook at Cacklefur Castle. He dreams of creating the ultimate stew.

Creepella's father, and the funeral director at Fabumouse Funerals.

The von Cacklefur family's meat-eating guard plant.

Geronimo Stilton

CREEPELLA VON CACKLEFUR

GHOST PIRATE TREASURE

Scholastic Inc.

New York   Toronto   London   Auckland
Sydney   Mexico City   New Delhi   Hong Kong

ISBN 978-0-545-30744-4

Copyright © 2010 by Edizioni Piemme S.p.A., Via Tiziano 32, 20145 Milan, Italy.

International Rights © Atlantyca S.p.A.

English translation © 2012 by Atlantyca S.p.A.

GERONIMO STILTON names, characters, and related indicia are copyright, trademark, and exclusive license of Atlantyca S.p.A. All rights reserved. The moral right of the author has been asserted.

Based on an original idea by Elisabetta Dami.

www.geronimostilton.com

Published by Scholastic Inc., 557 Broadway, New York, NY 10012. SCHOLASTIC and associated logos are trademarks and/or registered trademarks of Scholastic Inc.

Stilton is the name of a famous English cheese. It is a registered trademark of the Stilton Cheese Makers' Association. For more information, go to www.stiltoncheese.com.

Text by Geronimo Stilton
Original title Il tesoro del pirata fantasma
Cover by Giuseppe Ferrario
Illustrations by Ivan Bigarella (pencils and inks) and
Giulia Zaffaroni (color)
Graphics by Yuko Egusa

Special thanks to Tracey West
Translated by Lidia Morson Tramontozzi
Interior design by Elizabeth Frances Herzog

18 17 16   17/0

Printed in the U.S.A.   40

First printing, February 2012

A PACKAGE . . .
FROM THE SKY!

The streets in New Mouse City were dark and quiet when the clock struck midnight. Every mouse was snoring in bed, dreaming of cheese sandwiches. Almost every window in the city was shrouded in darkness. Only one light burned that night: MINE!

Oops! I almost forgot to tell you who I am. My name is Stilton, *Geronimo Stilton*. I run *The Rodent's Gazette*, the most famouse newspaper on Mouse Island.

My light was on because I was working late at the office on an **important** article. The subject matter of the article was making me a little nervous. Why? I'll tell you

the headline: **New Mouse City's Greatest Criminals**.

You see, I'm not the kind of mouse who's courageous. Even the names of those mean rats scare me silly. In fact, my tail goes limp when I just look at them: Barry Badguy, Roy the Rat Burglar, and Gary Gangster . . . **YIKES**!

I felt faint, so I opened the window to get some air. A gust of **WIND** cooled me off, and I lovingly looked down on my sleeping city.

Then I noticed dark clouds moving across the sky. The air became cold. Without warning, **HEAVY RAIN** poured down from above.

BARRY BADGUY

ROY THE RAT BURGLAR

GARY GANGSTER

I watched the rain fall, lost in thought, when suddenly . . .

BANG!

A package fell from the sky. I let out a frightened scream, held out my paws, and caught the package. Then I looked up to see who had dropped it and saw two tiny bat wings zigzagging away through the raindrops.

It was Bitewing, Creepella von Cacklefur's bat! I closed the window and opened the coffin-shaped package. Inside were a **NOTE**, a **NOTEBOOK**, and a moldy piece of

CHEESE that stunk like a sweaty sock after a football game! The note read:

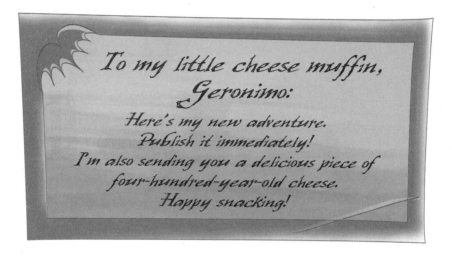

To my little cheese muffin,
Geronimo:
Here's my new adventure.
Publish it immediately!
I'm also sending you a delicious piece of
four-hundred-year-old cheese.
Happy snacking!

I was insulted. She expected me to eat a piece of cheese that was four centuries old? That STINKY stuff is unsafe to eat, unless you're a mummified mouse. Then again, I could always add it to my collection of antique cheese rinds.

I put the **PUTRID** cheese aside and picked up the notebook, which smelled just like the cheese. Even so, I kept reading until the sun came up.

It has an **AWFUL** *stench, but . . .* , I mused to myself.

My sister, Thea, a special correspondent at *The Rodent's Gazette,* interrupted my thoughts.

"What's that awful smell?" she squealed, walking into my office.

I gave her the notebook and she read the story.

"The notebook has a dreadful smell, but it's a **beautiful** story!" she said with admiration.

My nephew Benjamin and his friend Bugsy Wugsy read it next.

"It has a dreadful smell, but it's a **beautiful** story!" they both said.

My coworkers read it while pinching their noses.

"It has a dreadful smell, but it's a beautiful story!" they all agreed.

When my cousin Trap entered the office, he sniffed the air.

"What a DELIGHTFUL smell!" he exclaimed. Then he picked up the piece of cheese on my desk and ate it in one gulp! I think his stomach must be made of IRON.

Since everyone liked the story, I decided to publish Creepella's book. It is titled GHOST PIRATE TREASURE. You're holding it in your hot little paws right now. The only thing left for you to do is read it. I hope you like it as much as Trap enjoyed that stinky cheese!

GHOST PIRATE TREASURE

WRITTEN AND ILLUSTRATED BY
CREEPELLA VON CACKLEFUR

A DIFFICULT NIGHT

BILLY SQUEAKSPEARE was having another restless night. Every time he was about to doze off, one of the thirteen ghosts of Squeakspeare Mansion would burst in with some **RIDICULOUS** excuse.

At midnight, Miss Dustmop, the ghost housekeeper, threw open the door.

"This room needs a little extra **DUST**. I'll take care of it!" she said happily.

A moment later, Bob Woodmouse, the ghost **CARPENTER**, floated in.

"This isn't deep enough," he said, opening a desk drawer. "I'll make it deeper."

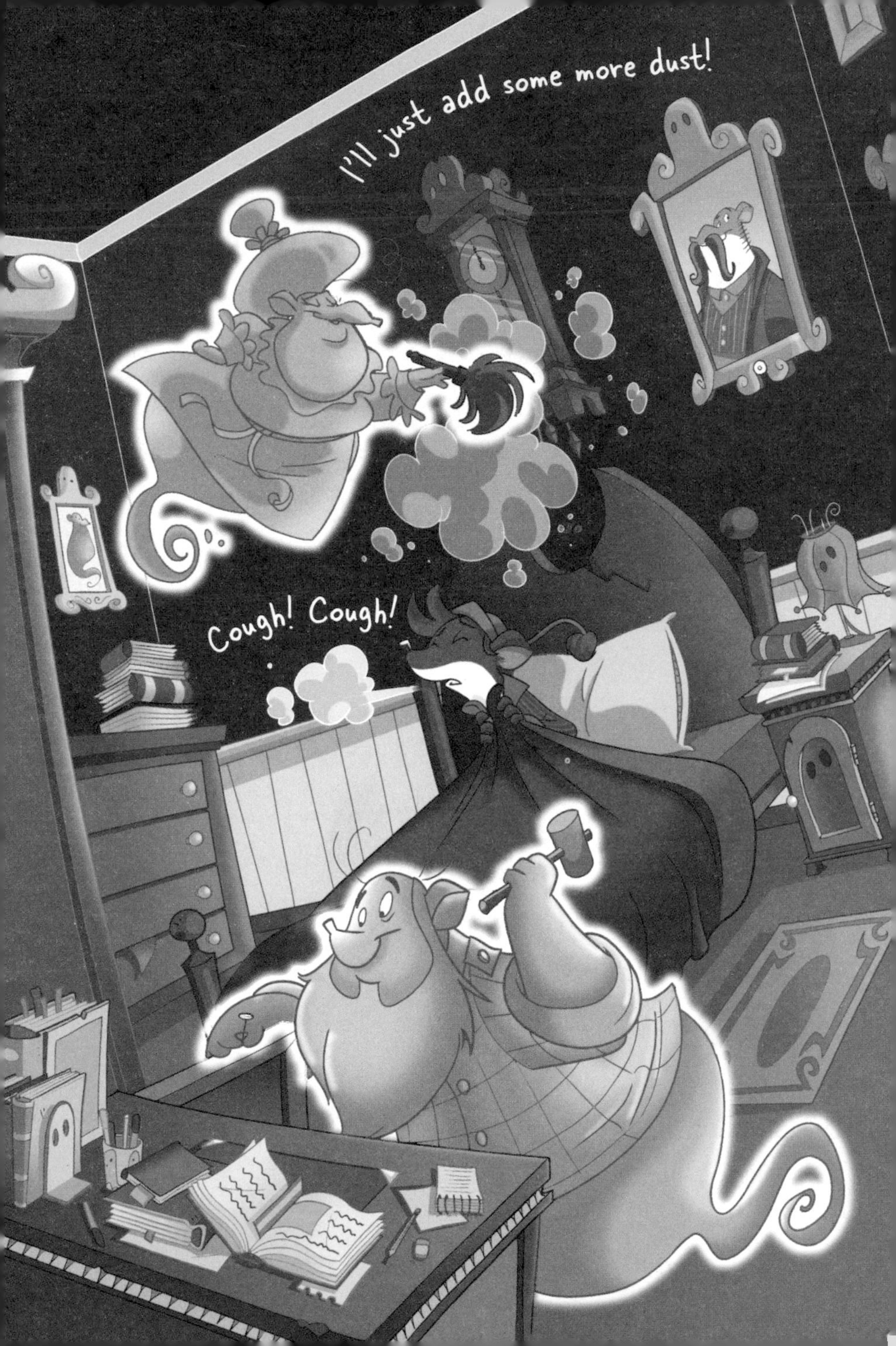
I'll just add some more dust!
Cough! Cough!

Between two and three **o'clock**, Dreamella
Airhead, the ghost maid, came in and
went out at least ten times.

"I can't find my **GLASSES**. They
must be here somewhere," she said.

She finally found them under Billy's
pillow.

Then, at three, Ted Trimmertail, the
ghost gardener, decided to **WATER** the
moss that grew under the night table.

At four o'clock, Arf, the
ghost dog, jumped on Billy's bed
and licked his face. Billy was
almost always grateful
for Arf's attention, but
not in the middle of the
night.

"Thank you, Arf, thank you," he said
with a yawn. "Now let me sleep!"

Arf seemed to understand. He curled up at the foot of the bed, closed his eyes, and began to doze off. A minute later, he raised his head and perked up his ears.

"**GRRRRRRRR!**" he growled. He was facing the yard.

Billy tried to calm him down. "Be a good boy, Arf," he said. "There's nobody there. Nobody!"

But Arf ran to the window. He barked and barked and barked.

Woof! Woof! Woooooooooooooof!

Billy got up and looked out the window. In the darkness of the night, the yard seemed peaceful and quiet. He went back to bed, but . . .

Woof! Woof! Woooooooooooooof!

"Arf, please be quiet!" Billy pleaded. In desperation, he tossed some items in Arf's direction to get his attention:

- a copy of **BLUE CHEESE AND A BLUE HEART**, the new book he was writing;

- an old, raggedy **SLIPPER**;

- an **alarm** clock;

- a **smelly** sock.

But Arf just kept **BARKING** and **BARKING**. Billy put a pillow over his ears and tried to sleep.

Finally, the first timid rays of sunlight appeared over the tops of the Mountains of the Mangy Yeti, jumped onto the Rancidrat River, and bounced into Billy's bedroom.

Billy sighed with relief. "It's about time!" he exclaimed. "Now my ghosts can all go to sleep. Even the dog!"

Billy snuggled under the covers, hoping to get just a few hours of sleep. He scratched his nose, closed his eyes, and was about to drift off when . . .

Vroom! Vroom! Vrooooom!

He sat up, listening. Outside, an engine was starting, stopping, and then starting again.

"Who would be here so early?" Billy asked himself worriedly.

He went to the window to see who was driving to his house at the crack of dawn. Instead, he saw a yard full of H⊙LES!

"Wh-wh-what?" he stammered.

Someone had dug big, deep H⊙LES all over his yard! The lawn looked like an enormouse piece of SWISS CHEESE. Billy scratched his head.

DO YOU KNOW THE ONE ABOUT THE PIRATE?

Dawn finally came and a tomblike SILENCE filled the mansion. The thirteen ghosts who lived there slept deeply during the day, just like any respectable ghost would. They had to recover from the **HARD WORK** they did at night.

Normally, Billy would be resting during those peaceful hours, too. But not that morning. Even though he was very tired, he couldn't stop twisting and turning in bed. He was wondering about the holes that had suddenly appeared in his yard.

Even counting the mansion's many **BATS** didn't help him fall asleep.

"I can't figure it out!" he blurted at bat number 1,264. "Maybe Uncle William can come up with an **explanation**."

Billy got dressed and walked down the hall. It was as quiet as an **EMPTY** tomb and as **cold** as the breath of the Abominable Snowrat. He got to the door of the boiler room and found it closed. A **WARNING** sign was nailed to the door.

DO NOT DISTURB!
GHOST
SLEEPING!

Billy stopped, unsure. Finally, he gathered his **courage** and entered the kingdom of his great-great-great-uncle *William Squeakspeare*. He found himself in a ROUND room with wall-to-wall bookcases filled with very OLD books.

His uncle was sound asleep in an old stuffed chair. His long whiskers were rolled up in **curlers**. Billy gently tried to wake him.

"U-Uncle William, w-w-wake up. S-something really **W-WEIRD** has happened."

But his uncle kept sleeping. Billy tried tickling his whiskers, but it didn't work. Finally, he took a deep breath and screamed as loudly as he could.

"UNCLE WILLIAM! WAKE UUUUUUP!"

The ghost jumped up like a spring. He waved his walking cane and stammered, "Wh-what happened? Is the house on fire? Is the enemy attacking? **Charge!**"

Then he noticed Billy and plopped himself down on the STUFFED chair.

Chaaaarge!

Uncle William, it's m—me!

"What happened, Nephew? Why did you disturb my sleep?" he asked.

"S-someone dug a l-lot of H◉LES in our yard last n-n-night," Billy stuttered.

Uncle William looked puzzled. He thought for a bit and then his face LIT UP.

"I've got it!" he cried. "They were probably looking for the treasure!"

Billy's whiskers trembled with excitement. "Treasure? Why would anyone l-l-look for t-t-treasure in our YARD?"

MORGAN BLACKWHISKERS

Uncle William yawned. "You really don't know much, do you, Nephew? Don't you know the LEGEND of Morgan Blackwhiskers, the pirate who stayed at our house and left us a treasure?"

"What?" Billy asked in disbelief.

His uncle nodded. As he continued his story, his eyes grew HEAVY with sleep. "If the gossips in Mysterious Valley were right, the pirate Blackwhiskers was a good friend to your great-great-great-grandmother Lady Squeakspeare. That was four hundred years ago, more or less."

LADY SQUEAKSPEARE

"Lady Squeakspeare?" Billy asked.

"Yes," his uncle replied, "but no one has ever found even a trace of the famouse treasure. And that's all I will tell you now, Nephew. It is time to sleep. But before I drift off, let me tell you some JOKES. Do you know the one about . . ."

He told a few jokes, but soon he fell into a **DEEP** sleep—as deep as a pot of cheese fondue.

Billy quietly slipped out of the room and gently shut the door. "Sweet dreams, Uncle!" he whispered.

"There's a real mystery afoot!" he exclaimed, scratching his nose. "And I know just the mouse who can help me solve it. I've got to call **CREEPELLA**!"

CREEPELLA, HELP ME!

"A layer of moldy-**MOSS** face powder . . . a light touch of snail-slime **lip gloss**. . . perfect! Just the right stuff to start the day."

Creepella von Cacklefur grinned at her reflection in the mirror as she got ready for work. She had a busy day ahead of her, interviewing a team of horror-movie makeup artists. She couldn't leave the house until her fur was the perfect pale shade of a MUMMY.

As she applied one last touch of shimmering caterpillar drool to her cheeks, her CELL PHONE rang.

"Hi, Creepella, it's B-B-Billy. Th-there's s-something worrying me."

"Dearest Billy-Willy, don't you worry," Creepella said.

"Why n-n-not?" Billy asked.

"Because your sweet Creepella has everything under control," she replied TRIUMPHANTLY.

"A-already?"

"Of course!" Creepella told him. "And they are splendidly horrid!"

"Well, that's good, then," Billy said, then stopped. "What are you t-talking about?"

"Why, I'm talking about our marvelous costumes, of course!" she said.

"C-costumes?" repeated Billy, baffled.

"Exactly! Costumes!" Creepella cried. "Lady Needletail did a fabumouse job!

For my rotted-flower costume, we had quite a discussion on the position of the petals. But your costume—"

"M-my costume?" Billy interrupted.

"Your costume is perfect," Creepella assured him. "You'll look great . . ."

"Wh-what?"

". . . dressed as a GARBAGE CAN!" she finished. "Wasn't that a truly DISGUSTING idea?"

"What are you talking about?" exclaimed a shocked Billy.

What did you say?

"What do you mean?" Creepella replied. "Didn't I tell you, dearest Billy? I asked the most fashionable designer in Mysterious Valley to have our costumes ready for tonight's GRAND BALL!"

"G-grand ball? Tonight?"

"Billy! Do I have to explain everything to you?" Creepella said with a sigh. "Today is the annual **Festival of Melancholy**, when all of Mysterious Valley celebrates the gloomiest day of the year. We'll start with a **supper** here at the castle and then go to the academy for the **MELANCHOLY GRAND BALL**."

"I d-don't know anything about it!" Billy insisted.

"**RATS** and **BATS**, Billy! Do you really want me to lose my patience?" Creepella snapped. "We all got our invitations weeks ago!"

Suddenly, Billy remembered. He searched furiously in his desk drawer and took out a very ELEGANT purple card.

His Excellency B. Squeakspeare is invited to the Melancholy Grand Ball. It will be held a fortnight from tonight at the Shivery Arts Academy.

Please remember: Everyone must wear a costume!

He had completely forgotten about it — probably because he didn't like parties much.

"Creepella, I don't think it's such a g-good idea," he stammered. "I'm not a g-good dancer."

"Nonsense! Don't say such FOOLISH things!" Creepella scolded. "There is no excuse to miss the MELANCHOLY GRAND BALL!"

Billy sighed. He knew he would never be able to change Creepella's mind.

"Fine, I'll come," he answered. "But before I do, you have to help me solve a mystery."

Creepella adored a good mystery. Her bright green eyes shone at the mention of the word.

"What is this mystery about, dearest Billy-Willy?" she asked eagerly.

"This morning I found the mansion's yard full of HOLES!" Billy explained. "Uncle William says that someone is looking for Morgan Blackwhiskers's treasure."

"Morgan Blackwhiskers! The most famouse pirate in Mysterious Valley?"

"That's the one!" Billy answered. "It seems he was a guest at Squeakspeare Mansion long ago."

"Billy, this sounds like an AWESOME mystery!" exclaimed Creepella. "We'll figure out who dug those holes . . . and with a little bit of luck, we'll also find the treasure!"

"Thanks, Creepella!" Billy said with relief. "I knew I could count on you."

Creepella ended the call and happily clapped her hands.

"This will be an absolutely spine-chilling horror story!" she cried. She turned to her pet bat, Bitewing, who was flying around her head.

"Bitewing, get ready! After breakfast, we need to solve a mystery!"

EMPTY BELLIES AT CACKLEFUR CASTLE

Creepella entered the dining room and found her whole **family** there. She quickly noticed that something very **weird** was going on. The **STRANGE** von Cacklefur family was acting even stranger than usual.

Her father, Boris, was pacing back and forth, mumbling. Poor Baby looked like he was going to CRY as he bounced on Madame LaTomb's knee. Chompers, the meat-eating plant, looked limp and weak. Creepella's niece Shivereen had an EMPTY look on her face. And the twins, Snip and Snap, weren't playing any tricks as usual. Instead, they looked SAD.

"What's the matter?" asked Creepella.

"It's a **TRAGEDY**!" Grandma Crypt answered. "Chef Stewrat didn't make the stew for breakfast!"

Creepella was shocked. Chef Stewrat served the same thing at every meal: a big pot of stew made from ingredients that only the von Cacklefurs could appreciate (and digest)!

Chef Stewrat **BURST** into the room. "**I'M RUINED!**" he cried. "My cooking career is over! Tonight everyone is supposed to prepare something special for the **MELANCHOLY GRAND BALL**. But I just can't do it!"

"I'm covering the furniture with silver COBWEBS," interrupted Grandma Crypt.

"We have trick candles for the Melancholy Cake," said Snip and Snap.

Boris nodded. "I've composed a poem called

'Dark and Dreary Tombs'

to be read before dinner," he said.

"Dinner! That's my problem!" exclaimed Chef Stewrat. "You see, I want to make an extra-SPECIAL stew for the dinner tonight."

"I think that's an EXCELLENT idea," Creepella said encouragingly.

"Yes, but to make a SPECIAL stew, I need an extra-SPECIAL ingredient," whined Chef Stewrat. "I have tried everything, but nothing is working. If I can't make a SPECIAL stew, I'm sunk."

He handed Creepella a piece of oil-stained paper.

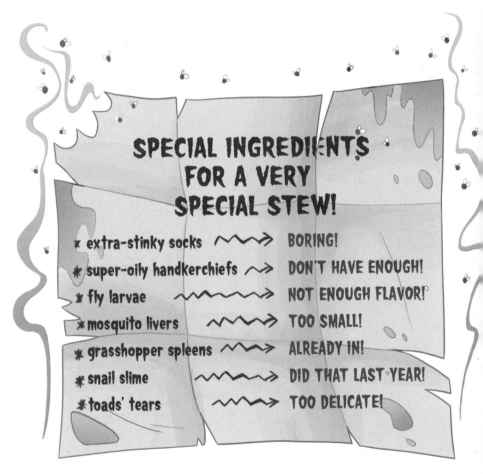

SPECIAL INGREDIENTS FOR A VERY SPECIAL STEW!

* extra-stinky socks ～～～> BORING!
* super-oily handkerchiefs ～～> DON'T HAVE ENOUGH!
* fly larvae ～～～～> NOT ENOUGH FLAVOR!
* mosquito livers ～～～> TOO SMALL!
* grasshopper spleens ～～> ALREADY IN!
* snail slime ～～～> DID THAT LAST YEAR!
* toads' tears ～～～> TOO DELICATE!

Creepella tried to **CHEER** him up. "Don't worry, Chef Stewrat. I'll find you the right ingredient," she said.

"Really?" he asked, wiping a TEAR from his eye.

You'll really help me?

"Of course!" she replied. "In the meantime, why don't you make us a DELICIOUSLY DISGUSTING breakfast stew? We von Cacklefurs can't live without it!"

HUNTING FOR CLUES!

Creepella had to hurry, or she would be late for her meeting with Billy. She **RAN** to the door but bumped into something in the hallway.

"Who left a **pillow** in the middle of the hall?" she asked.

"That's not a pillow," said Shivereen. "It's **Kafka**!"

The von Cacklefur family's pet cockroach lay on its back on the floor with its legs in the air. Its tummy was so **SWOLLEN** it looked like a feather-stuffed pillow.

Creepella knelt down next to the cockroach. "Poor Kafka. What's wrong?"

"He's got **INDIGESTION**," Shivereen explained. She held up a box with the words

on it. "I wanted to give him a treat, but he gobbled the whole box in one bite!"

Creepella shook her head. "You've got such a **sweet TOOTH**, Kafka! Get up and get moving and you'll feel better soon."

Moments later they were all in Creepella's **Turborapid 3000**, zooming toward Billy's mansion. They found him in the yard, surrounded by holes.

Kafka crawled around, sniffing. Shivereen

started snapping PHOTOS. Creepella examined the holes as Bitewing flew around her head.

"Very interesting," she remarked. "They look like they were **DUG** by a professional."

"Wh-what makes you say that?" Billy asked.

"I took a class on mysterious wells, holes, and tunnels at the Shivery Arts Academy," Creepella explained. "The holes are all the same size, and the **ROCKS** are piled neatly beside each other. That's the mark of a real pro."

"Could the digger be d-d-dangerous?" Billy asked, his whiskers trembling.

"Of course!" teased Bitewing.

Creepella decided to have a little fun with her friend Billy.

"You are in graaaaave daaaaanger!"

she said in a spooky voice.

"D-d-danger?" Billy looked faint.

"Just kidding!" Creepella said. "This night digger is **MYSTERIOUS**, that's all. Now come with me!"

"Where are we g-g-going?" whispered Billy.

"To the Shivery Arts Academy!" she replied. "Somebody must be looking for **Morgan Blackwhiskers's** treasure. If we want to beat him to it, we've got to learn more about the treasure. And I know exactly who can help us!"

"Auntie, maybe I should stay here with Kafka," Shivereen piped up. "He doesn't look well."

Kafka was on his back again, groaning with a **TUMMY ACHE**.

"Good idea, but loan me your camera," Creepella said. "Those PHOTOS you took might be helpful."

Then Creepella, Billy, and Bitewing **sped away** in the purple hearse.

What nobody knew, however, was that some spies behind a bush were **WATCHING** their every move. . . .

? Who's hiding behind the bush?

INVESTIGATION AT THE ACADEMY

Creepella's car **SCREECHED** to a stop in front of the **SHIVERY ARTS ACADEMY**.

"The first stop is Professor Dubloon's office!" she exclaimed.

"Who's th-that?" asked Billy timidly.

"He teaches **pirate history**," explained Creepella. "He's an expert on just about everything there is to know about the **pirates** who sailed the seas."

Excited, Creepella grabbed Billy by the paw and *DRAGGED* him through the halls of the academy. Finally, they stopped at a door with a **PLAQUE** on the front.

Professor Dubloon
FIRST-CLASS PIRATOLOGIST
EXPERT ON THE HISTORY OF PIRATES,
PRIVATEERS, AND BUCCANEERS

Creepella was about to knock on the door when it opened by itself. A friendly-looking face with a black **patch** over one eye peeked out.

"Are you here already?" asked the old rodent. He lifted his strange-looking **HAT** in greeting. "I didn't expect you so soon!"

"Y-you were waiting for us?" asked Billy.

"Of course!" Dubloon replied. "It's not every day that one gets to meet such an important pair of scholars."

"Sch-scholars? What do you m-mean?" Billy asked **suspiciously**.

Dubloon frowned. "Aren't you the Syllable Sisters, the famouse interpreters of pirate language?"

"Professor, you're such a **KIDDER**!" laughed Creepella.

"Trumpeting treasures! I know that voice. It's Creepella!" the professor exclaimed, lifting his eye patch. Then he ran toward Billy.

"Actually, you do look a little **DIFFERENT**," Dubloon said.

"*Th-that's* Creepella," Billy said, pointing.

"Of course!" the professor exclaimed, turning to Creepella. He winked at her. "Then who is this less glamorous friend of yours?"

"That's Billy Squeakspeare, the *writer*!" Bitewing piped up.

Professor Dubloon looked EXCITED. "Wondrous whales! A writer! He's brought me an awesome pirate's biography, hasn't he?"

"Actually, we're here because we need to learn about the pirate **Morgan Blackwhiskers**," Creepella explained. "It seems he hid his treasure in my friend's yard years ago. Do you know anything about it?"

"Hmm, let's see," he replied. "Blackwhiskers, you say?"

Creepella and Billy followed the professor into his office. Strange OLD OBJECTS crowded the bookshelves. A YELLOWED sheet of paper was pinned to the wall.

OFFICE INVENTORY

- 24 encyclopedias about piracy
- 12 essays about pirate raids, attacks, and abandoned ships
- 117 ships' diaries of famouse pirates
- 113 old flags from pirate ships
- 44 maps of treasures found by others
- 8 hooks from history's most feared pirates
- 3 colored feathers from Surly Sam, the most famous pirate parrot
- 1 extremely rare treasure-finder compass (broken)

The professor RUMMAGED through the volumes of old, dusty books until he finally found what he was looking for.

"Ah, here it is!" Dubloon cried. "According to the **Encyclopedia of Pirate Journeys**, Blackwhiskers passed through the Mysterious Valley and was a guest at Squeakspeare Mansion."

Creepella nudged Billy. "You see? We came to the right place!"

Dubloon kept reading. "Because he was somewhat of a gentlemouse, Blackwhiskers gave a GIFT to his hostess, the beautiful Lady Squeakspeare. It was a treasure from one of his pirate raids."

"D-d-does anyone know where it's h-h-hidden?" asked Billy hopefully.

The professor shook his head. "No, my dear writer. NO ONE knows."

"So the only one who would know exactly where Blackwhiskers buried his treasure would be . . . his ghost?" Creepella asked.

"Unfortunately, Blackwhiskers was the most **FORGETFUL** pirate in history," Dubloon said. "Once he **BURIED** his treasures, he immediately forgot where he had put them!"

"Then it very well could have been his ghost who **DUG** all of those holes in the yard!" Creepella said, her voice growing louder with excitement. "What a great story! A mysterious treasure, a **pirate**, and a ghost, all in one! I'll write the greatest scoop of the century!"

Professor Dubloon frowned. "Well, if my

studies are correct, then Blackwhiskers can't be the digger," he said. "In fact, his ghost can only appear after the treasure is found. That's according to every legend I've ever read."

Billy was DISCOURAGED. "Then there's no solution," he said with a sigh.

But Creepella wasn't disappointed. "Don't worry, Billy-Willy, we'll find the treasure," she promised. "Then the ghost of that famouse pirate will appear and I'll get my SCOOP. All we need to do is figure out who is digging up your yard!"

ADVICE AND HIDING PLACES

Creepella **DASHED** out of the office without even saying good-bye to Professor Dubloon. Billy followed.

"Creep . . . Creepella, where are we *going*?" he asked.

"To see Professor Cleverpaws, of course!" she replied.

"Another p-p-pirate **expert**?" Billy asked.

Creepella shook her head. "No, we don't need another pirate expert right now," she said. "We need to *Discover* who dug those holes! They are the KEY to this mystery."

Creepella began to climb the **MOLDY** steps that led to the top of a tall turret. "Professor Cleverpaws is an expert on hiding places," she explained. "I want to show her a P H O T O of the holes. Maybe she can figure out who dug them."

THE HOLES ARE THE KEY!

Pant! Pant!

When they reached the top of the steps, Billy read the  **PLAQUE** on the door:

Professor Cleverpaws
DISCOVERER AND ANALYST OF HIDING PLACES OF ALL KINDS
EXPERT FOLLOWER OF TRAILS,
TRACKS, AND PAWPRINTS

"I was her best student," Creepella revealed proudly before knocking on the door.

"Who's there?" asked a voice from inside. An instant later, an **ATHLETIC**-looking rodent opened the door. She wore a **HUGE** pair of binoculars around her neck.

"Creepella, is that you?" she asked. "My *exceptional* snooper student! Are you here to do some research? And is this your assistant?"

"Actually, I'm B-B-Billy Squeakspeare," Billy told her. "I'm a writer."

"Nice to meet you," said the professor. "Come in."

Creepella and Billy followed the professor into her study. The room was filled with binoculars, flashlights, and other instruments that could be used to search for hidden places.

"We're looking for a treasure," Creepella explained. "But we're not the only ones looking for it. I believe a professional digger is after the treasure."

Creepella handed Shivereen's camera to the professor. Professor Cleverpaws zoomed in on a photo and examined it carefully.

"Hmm, you're right!" she said finally. "This is the work of a PROFESSIONAL—and I think I know who it is!"

Mission Incomplete!

Back at Squeakspeare Mansion, Kafka the cockroach was still groaning from his tummy ache. Shivereen felt sorry for the poor bug, so she decided to tell him a story.

"Once upon a time, there was a big spider. It lived all by itself in the cemetery, inside the **TRUNK** of an old tree. . . ."

"They're wrapped up in the story," WHISPERED a voice from behind the bushes. "Let's go now!"

Then Tilly, Milly, and Lilly, the Rattenbaum triplets, tiptoed out from behind the bush. Something else FOLLOWED them, moving very slowly. The leaves crackled under the creature's many feet.

"Ziggy, be quiet!" Tilly hissed at the creature—a large **millipede**, which followed the girls wherever they went.

Ziggy the Millipede

The triplets hopped into their old, beat-up car. Ziggy slowly climbed into the backseat, and Milly *SPED* away. Soon the shadow of Rattenbaum Mansion loomed on the horizon. The formerly grand house looked like it was falling apart.

"I knew it! He's here," said Tilly.

"I knew it! He's waiting!" added Milly.

"I knew it! What now?" asked Lilly.

At the gate of the old building stood the odd shape of Shamley Rattenbaum, as still as a statue. He wore a TATTERED suit and

a collapsed top hat. When he saw the triplets, he opened his arms wide.

"My SOPHISTICATED, lovely, enchanting granddaughters!" he cried. "What good news have you brought your grandfather today?"

I knew it!
He's waiting!
What now?

THATAWAY

THIS WAY

MORE OR LESS

The triplets *slowly* got out of the car, but none of the girls answered him.

"My dearest triplets, please tell me," Shamley said. "Mission accomplished?"

"Actually . . . ," began Tilly.

". . . mission . . . ," continued Milly.

". . . incomplete!" finished Lilly.

"WHAT DID YOU SAY?" Shamley roared furiously. "YOU DIDN'T FIND THE TREASURE?!?"

The triplets HUDDLED together.

"No treasure," said Tilly finally.

Milly chimed in. "In fact, we found . . ."

You didn't find the treasure?

". . . only an empty can," finished Lilly.

"Unbelievable!" cried Shamley. "Ziggy is a professional digger. How could you have failed?"

Tilly, Milly, and Lilly defended themselves. "We worked all night!"

"Maybe that story you heard is false!"

"Maybe the truth is that there is no treasure!"

Shamley got angry. "What do you mean it's not true? A respectable GENTLEMOUSE at the Snob Society Rodents' Club told me the tale! He said that Morgan Blackwhiskers left a treasure there for Lady Squeakspeare."

"Then maybe someone else found it," Milly suggested.

"Impossible! We would have heard about it," Shamley pointed out. "Now go back to Squeakspeare Mansion and keep looking!"

The triplets tried to protest.

"But ..."

"No ..."

"If ..."

Their grandfather cut them short. "No excuses! Get moving, and don't come back with empty 🐾🐾🐾🐾! We can't invite anyone over for a high-society feast unless we can make some . . . *ahem* . . . *minor* repairs to the mansion."

Ziggy the Millipede

JOB: Official companion to the Rattenbaum triplets

ORIGINAL HOME: The Moccasin Mountains

AGE: Old enough to buy shoes in adult sizes

NOTABLE QUIRKS: He has several thousand pairs of shoes.

FAVORITES: He enjoys designer footwear, but he'll buy shoes on sale if they're comfortable.

STYLES: In the summer, he wears clogs, sandals, and flip-flops. In the winter, he wears wool socks and ski boots. At home, he always wears slippers.

STRENGTHS: He is an excellent digger and he always finishes a job.

WEAKNESSES: He has a short attention span and tires easily.

A Very Crowded Garden

Back at the academy, Professor Cleverpaws had identified the digger immediately: Ziggy the **millipede**, her ex-assistant. Ziggy had left the academy to work for the Rattenbaums.

"It looks like those **BRATTY** triplets are behind this mystery!" Creepella exclaimed as she and Billy walked back to the hearse. "Billy, let's go back to your mansion. We have to find the treasure before those three do. I want to be the first to see **Blackwhiskers** appear!"

The **Turborapid 3000** roared into

Billy's driveway right as the Rattenbaums' old car pulled up, trailing big *puffs* of gray exhaust.

"Rats and bats!" Creepella said with a frown. "Those snobby pretenders are here already!"

The *triplets* immediately circled Billy, showering him with fake compliments.

"Well, well," said Creepella, eyeing them carefully. "What brings you here?"

The three mice barely looked up.

"Ugh! The *annoying* one is here, too," said Tilly.

"So *irritating!*" added Milly.

"And *creepy!*" Lilly said.

"Of course I'm here," Creepella snapped. "And I've got some news about a certain hole digger you know."

The triplets looked *ALARMED*.

"We don't know —"

"— what —"

"— you're talking about!"

At that moment, Ziggy crawled out of their car, looking sleepier than ever.

"There he is!" Creepella cried, pointing to the **millipede**. "He dug all of the holes in Billy's yard!"

"Nonsense!" insisted Milly. "He's **Ziggy**, our pet millipede."

"He doesn't know anything about your H⚫LES!" Tilly blurted out.

"Besides, you don't have any proof!" declared Lilly.

"I'm **SURE** you three are behind this!" Creepella argued. "And now you've come back to dig some more! That's stealing, you know."

"Absolutely not!" Tilly cried. "We're here to invite Billy—"

"—to be our date—" continued Milly.

"—to the Melancholy Grand Ball!" finished Lilly.

Creepella got angry again. "Back off! Everybody knows that Billy is escorting **ME** to the ball!"

Shivereen ran up before an argument could begin. "There you are, Auntie. Kafka is much better. Look!"

The von Cacklefur **cockroach** was **trotting** all over the yard, happy to be feeling better. He was having fun **exploring** the holes, and his tummy didn't hurt anymore. In fact, he was hungry. He sniffed around for something to **MUNCH** on.

Kafka came out of a hole with something in his mouth—but it wasn't something he

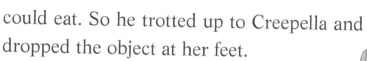

could eat. So he trotted up to Creepella and
dropped the object at her feet.

"ARF ARF ARF!"

Kafka barked.

What did you find, Kafka?

THE HOLE DIGGER UNMASKED

The object that Kafka placed at Creepella's feet was not a TWIG. She picked it up and examined it.

"Rats and bats!" she exclaimed. "This is a LITTLE SHOE!"

"What would a shoe be doing in my yard?" asked Billy.

The triplets exchanged nervous glances and quickly walked BACKWARD.

Creepella picked up Kafka. "Where did you find it, little one?" she asked him.

Kafka pointed one of his antennae at the deepest hole in the yard.

"ARF ARF ARF!"

Bitewing translated for Billy, who was the only one who didn't understand Arfese, Kafka's language.

"He found it in that hole down there," the bat said.

Creepella placed Kafka back on the ground and examined the shoe with the eye of a detective. She brushed the dirt off it to reveal a number on the sole: **822**.

Creepella approached the millipede. Ziggy was as pale as a ghost and trembling like a dry leaf.

"**Zigi zigizi zig zig?**" Creepella asked in millipede language.

"Zigi, zigi, zig. Zigzig," mumbled Ziggy.

Creepella gave him a kind smile. "Ziggi!"

Billy was AMAZED. "Creepella, you understand him?"

"Of course!" she replied. "Everybody knows Millipedese. And look here. . . ."

Creepella gently turned Ziggy onto his BACK and began to count the numbers on the soles of his little shoes.

"Eight hundred twenty . . . eight hundred twenty-one . . . Look here, what a coincidence! His missing shoe is number eight hundred twenty-two!" she exclaimed, pointing to one tiny bare foot.

Meanwhile, the triplets were trying to make a hasty RETREAT to their car.

Shivereen noticed their attempted escape.

"Look, Auntie, the Rattenbaums are getting away!" she cried.

"Stop right there!" Creepella shouted. "This shoe is proof that your **millipede** dug all of these holes. Poor thing! He told me that you promised you'd increase his food to a full loaf of **MOLDY** bread a day. Tell me, what were you looking for? Perhaps . . . a treasure?"

"How dare you!" protested Milly.

"Ziggy must have done it all on his own," said Tilly.

"We don't know anything about pirate loot," added Lilly.

Creepella crossed her arms and **smiled** slyly. "Why did you use the word **Pirate**?" she asked. "I didn't say anything about pirates!"

The three mice turned as PALE as mozzarella. They picked up Ziggy and shoved him into the backseat of the car.

"Let's get away from this riffraff!"

"Accusing us of digging holes!"

"We have better things to do!"

"How do you think Grandfather will take it?" asked Tilly as she climbed into the car.

"This means there will be no feast before tonight's MELANCHOLY GRAND BALL," added Lilly.

"And no one will want to escort us to the GRAND BALL, either," sighed Milly.

WHERE'S THE TREASURE?

The Rattenbaums' car STALLED and sputtered. Shivereen had time to talk to Ziggy through the window.

"Here, take this!" she whispered, handing him a small package. "It's Kafka's candy. He's very happy to give it to you. Besides, you didn't realize you were doing anything WRONG!"

"Zigziggi!" gurgled Ziggy gratefully. Then he licked Shivereen's nose.

"Those three are so dishonest," said Creepella as the car drove off, shooting out puffs of smoke. "At least they won't be able to find the treasure!"

Hee hee! That tickles!

Bitewing flew around her head. "By the way . . . where's the treasure? Where's the treasure? Where's the treasure?"

Creepella thoughtfully **twirled** a strand of her long black hair around her finger. She began walking around the garden, talking out loud.

"Maybe they were looking in the **WRONG** place," she mused. "But Blackwhiskers always buried his treasures, right?"

Shivereen and Billy nodded.

"Then the YARD must be where the treasure is hidden," Creepella reasoned. "Maybe the holes weren't deep enough."

Billy moved to follow her, but he tripped in a H◎LE. He fell into a big old fountain

Heeeeelp!

hidden by a prickly thornbush, landing in the MURKY water.

Splash!

"Oh, Billy, you can be so CLUMSY sometimes!" Creepella scolded him.

"Silly Billy!" Bitewing teased.

Billy climbed out of the fountain, dripping wet. "Actually, there's s-s-something —"

"QUIET, please, Billy," Creepella said. "I'm trying to think!"

"B-b-b-but I see s-s-s-something under —" Billy stammered.

Shivereen interrupted him this time. She pointed to the top of his head.

"What's that on your head? A frog?"

"A frog . . . with a gold coin in its mouth!" Creepella announced, shocked. She

carefully climbed into the fountain and felt along the **BOTTOM** with her paw.

"Just as I thought!" she cried. "There's something **peculiar** under here!"

"Th-th-that's exactly what I've been trying to t-t-tell you," Billy said, but Creepella wasn't listening. With a sigh, Billy reached into the fountain and pulled up a **heavy** old treasure chest made of **METAL**.

"I was right!" Creepella cried.

"The treasure! The treasure of Morgan Blackwhiskers!"

"Stop talking and open it up!" Bitewing urged impatiently.

WHAT A FORTUNE, THIS FORTUNE!

"Yes, please open it!" Shivereen said eagerly.

Creepella forced open the RUSTY old lock. The lid creaked as she lifted it up.

"Rats and bats!" she cried. "There's a fortune inside!"

Gold coins overflowed from the chest. Each one was stamped with the image of a gentlemouse wearing a WIG and crown.

"Who's the dude on the coin?" asked Shivereen.

"King Mousard the Fourth," answered Creepella. "He ruled Mysterious Valley four hundred years ago."

Bitewing took one of the coins and bit it. "**OUCH!** There's no doubt. It's made of gold! Wonderful gold!"

Creepella pulled a yellowed sheet of paper out of the chest. She read it out loud.

I gathered this bounty of coins during my many pirate adventures. I would like to give all of it to the lovely, delicate, and adorable Lady Squeakspeare as a token of thanks. She gladdened the later years of my life with her precious friendship.

Morgan Blackwhiskers

"How **ROMANTIC!**" sighed Shivereen, drying a tear.

"There's something else written, but it's hard to read," Creepella said, frowning. She **wrinkled** her nose and continued.

I forgot! Old age has dimmed my memory. I can never remember where I hide my things!
If Lady Squeakspeare doesn't find this chest, the treasure will be inherited by her grandchildren. Or her great-grandchildren. Or her great-great-great-grandchildren. Or whomever finds it—as long as that mouse bears the Squeakspeare name!

"Did you hear, Billy?" Shivereen asked, her voice rising with excitement. "The treasure is yours!"

"I c-c-can't believe it!" Billy stammered, turning red.

"Of course, all of these coins were STOLEN by Blackwhiskers all those years ago," Creepella pointed out. "And since there is no way to return them, you'll simply have to give the money away."

"B-b-but . . . ," Billy protested.

"I suggest that you set up a scholarship for young deserving rodents at the Shivery Arts Academy," she said, ignoring him.

Billy sighed. He knew in his heart that Creepella was right.

"You could also put up a STATUE of Morgan Blackwhiskers in Gloomeria

GREETINGS FROM THE PIRATES OF GLOOMERIA!

M.B.

Square," Creepella went on. "I think Lady Squeakspeare would have liked that."

"It's a great idea," Billy said reluctantly.

Bitewing flew around the chest, curious. "Do any of you smell something **peculiar**?"

Creepella sniffed the air. "You're right!" she agreed. "That box has a heavenly smell. Maybe there's something underneath the coins."

She plunged her paw into the coins and took out a YELLOWISH OBJECT covered in green mold. The smell was so strong that Billy **fainted** on the spot.

But Creepella adored the odor. "It's cheese aged to perfection. I'd say it's aged for at least four hundred years!"

"Look how BEAUTIFULLY MOLDY it is!" Shivereen exclaimed.

Billy woke up feeling wobbly and queasy. "I'd say it's MONSTEROUSLY MOLDY!" he said.

Then a little worm popped out of the CHEESE. He looked very old, and he had a long beard and glasses.

Old worm

"What's that?" whimpered Billy nervously.

"It's an OLD WORM, of course!" Creepella

answered. "Hmm. I wonder if this cheese is just what Chef Stewrat needs."

"Hooray!" cheered Shivereen. "It's the extra-special ingredient for his **SPECIAL MELANCHOLY STEW!**"

"B-b-but do you really think that eating cheese that's f-f-four hundred years old is a good idea?" stuttered Billy, holding his nose closed.

"Of course!" Creepella replied. "Let's bring it to him *pronto*!"

A HORRIDLY DELIGHTFUL DINNER

"SUPERB! SUBLIME! SUPER!"

exclaimed Chef Stewrat after he tasted a crumb of the moldy aɴᴛɪǫᴜᴇ ᴄʜᴇᴇsᴇ. The disgusting stench of the cheese soon spread through the castle, making the residents FEROCIOUSLY hungry.

"Hold up, Chompers!" warned Creepella as the meat-eating plant dove into the **BUBBLING** stew with a spoon. "That stew is for tonight's feast!"

That night, everyone in Cacklefur Castle got ready for dinner. The ancient building had never looked so **GLOOMY**. Grandmother Crypt had covered the furniture with shimmering cobwebs, giving the room a beautiful *ghostly* look.

Before sitting down to the feast, Boris von Cacklefur read his poem, "Dark and Dreary Tombs."

Dark and Dreary Tombs

by Boris von Cacklefur, famouse poet

❧ ❧ ❧

Oh, dark and dreary tombs,
Stinky is your smell.
Any mouse who enters
Will not long there dwell.
Dusty and dreary,
And yet so delightful,
Damp, dank, and dark,
Full of horrors so frightful!
Oh, dark and dreary tombs,
Resting place of mice,
No place on Earth
Is so dreadfully nice!

"What a poet!"
"What a genius!"
"What a wordsmith!"

Everyone praised Boris's poem. Then they all dug in to Chef Stewrat's **SPECIAL MELANCHOLY STEW**.

But when Billy had his first bite, he immediately turned green and started to feel sick and QUEASY.

"Excuse me, please," he said, standing up. "I really don't feel well at all."

"Don't be modest, Billy. You look GREAT!" Creepella exclaimed. "That green will match your costume perfectly. Now let's get ready for the ball!"

Billy and Creepella changed into their costumes. They looked GHASTLY.

"You two look fabumousely FRIGHTENING," declared Shivereen.

A Surprising Guest

Billy was having a hard time moving around in his **GARBAGE CAN** costume. He **TRIPPED** three times trying to jump inside the *Turborapid 3000*.

"Billy, you look *fantastic* as a garbage can!" Creepella said as she took off at top speed.

The entrance to the Shivery Arts Academy was draped with purple funeral lights and flickering lamps.

"What a **DELIGHTFULLY DREARY** party!" Creepella whispered dreamily.

The courtyard was overflowing with **costumed** rodents. They were dressed as mummies, vampires, witches, ghosts, ghouls, various monsters—and one garbage can.

The Rattenbaum triplets were there, too. They tried to look glamorous, but instead, they looked **comical**. Milly's dress was too long, Tilly's was too short, and Lilly's was too large. Pesky little spiders dangled from their wigs, *tickling* their snouts. Ziggy, the millipede, came with them, and he wore a tap shoe on each of his one thousand tiny little feet!

"What a heavenly sight!"

cooed Creepella.

Poor Billy didn't agree. The guests kept dumping their garbage into his costume. The can got so **HEAVY** that he couldn't move!

He sat on a bench and watched Creepella dance with Ziggy. Finally, Creepella came back to him.

"It's an **unforgettable** party," she sighed. Then she frowned. "There's only one thing missing: the visit of a nice ghost I could interview. I wonder what Blackwhiskers is waiting for. We've found the treasure. Isn't he supposed to appear?"

Suddenly, a cold wind whipped around Creepella and Billy. Then a ghost with a long black MUSTACHE and a black BEARD appeared in front of them. It was Morgan Blackwhiskers.

"I heard that somebody took my treasure,"

he said crossly. "Who is it?"

Creepella clapped her paws with happiness. "Mr. Blackwhiskers! It was my Billy who found your treasure. Right, Billy?"

But poor Billy had **fainted**. He was sprawled on the ground, surrounded by all the **GARBAGE** from his costume.

"Billy, why do you always faint just when things get **EXCITING**?" Creepella asked, shaking her head. Then she turned to the **pirate** ghost. "That's Billy Squeakspeare. He is related to your **FRIEND** Lady Squeakspeare."

"A Squeakspeare?" exclaimed the ghost, remembering everything. "Then my treasure is in good paws!"

"Of course!" declared Creepella. "Now, can we go somewhere a little more quiet, **Mr. Blackwhiskers**? I'd like to have a nice interview with you!"

THE END

ANOTHER BESTSELLER

Once again, Creepella's new book got rave reviews.

Fans from all over sent **letters**, text messages, and e-mails, and made phone calls to *The Rodent's Gazette*, asking for another **HORROR** story right away.

Can you believe the book's biggest **Fan** was my grandfather William Shortpaws? One morning he **BURST** into my office, thundering, "Don't be such a lazybones, Grandson! What are you waiting for? When will you publish Creepella von Cacklefur's next **book**? She is the most awesome **HORROR** novelist in all of Mysterious Valley."

"I don't have a clue," I told him. "I never know when my friend will drop a book on my desk."

But my grandfather kept asking me when the next book would come out. He *called* me five times a day! And when Benjamin and Bugsy Wugsy visited me in my office, they seemed **DiSaPPOiNteD** that I didn't have a new **CREEPELLA** story for them. Even the little mouselets who came to buy Creepella's books asked the same question. I finally decided to send my friend this **MESSAGE**:

Write, Creepella! Write, write, write! We're all waiting for your new bestseller!

Geronimo Stilton,
Editor of *The Rodent's Gazette*

If you liked this book, be sure
to check out my next adventure!

RETURN OF THE VAMPIRE

A mysterious old friend of Grandpa Frankenstein shows up one night on the doorstep of Cacklefur Castle. He's a vampire . . . and he's seeking the von Cacklefur family's help. His castle has been infested by strange and troublesome monsters and ghosts, and he's afraid he'll have to move out because of them! Yikes! It's up to Creepella and her family and friends to help this vampire save his home.

And don't miss any of my other fabumouse adventures!

#1 Lost Treasure of the Emerald Eye

#2 The Curse of the Cheese Pyramid

#3 Cat and Mouse in a Haunted House

#4 I'm Too Fond of My Fur!

#5 Four Mice Deep in the Jungle

#6 Paws Off, Cheddarface!

#7 Red Pizzas for a Blue Count

#8 Attack of the Bandit Cats

#9 A Fabumouse Vacation for Geronimo

#10 All Because of a Cup of Coffee

#11 It's Halloween, You 'Fraidy Mouse!

#12 Merry Christmas, Geronimo!

#13 The Phantom of the Subway

#14 The Temple of the Ruby of Fire

#15 The Mona Mousa Code

#16 A Cheese-Colored Camper

#17 Watch Your Whiskers, Stilton!

#18 Shipwreck on the Pirate Islands

#19 My Name Is Stilton, Geronimo Stilton   **#20 Surf's Up, Geronimo!**   **#21 The Wild, Wild West**   **#22 The Secret of Cacklefur Castle**   **A Christmas Tale**

#23 Valentine's Day Disaster   **#24 Field Trip to Niagara Falls**   **#25 The Search for Sunken Treasure**   **#26 The Mummy with No Name**   **#27 The Christmas Toy Factory**

#28 Wedding Crasher   **#29 Down and Out Down Under**   **#30 The Mouse Island Marathon**   **#31 The Mysterious Cheese Thief**   **Christmas Catastrophe**

#32 Valley of the Giant Skeletons   **#33 Geronimo and the Gold Medal Mystery**   **#34 Geronimo Stilton, Secret Agent**   **#35 A Very Merry Christmas**   **#36 Geronimo's Valentine**

#37 The Race Across America

#38 A Fabumouse School Adventure

#39 Singing Sensation

#40 The Karate Mouse

#41 Mighty Mount Kilimanjaro

#42 The Peculiar Pumpkin Thief

#43 I'm Not a Supermouse!

#44 The Giant Diamond Robbery

#45 Save the White Whale!

#46 The Haunted Castle

#47 Run for the Hills, Geronimo!

#48 The Mystery in Venice

And coming soon!

#49 The Way of the Samurai

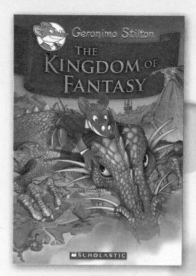

THE KINGDOM OF FANTASY

THE QUEST FOR PARADISE:
THE RETURN TO THE KINGDOM OF FANTASY

THE AMAZING VOYAGE:
THE THIRD ADVENTURE IN THE KINGDOM OF FANTASY

Be sure to check out these exciting Thea Sisters adventures!

THEA STILTON AND THE DRAGON'S CODE

THEA STILTON AND THE MOUNTAIN OF FIRE

THEA STILTON AND THE GHOST OF THE SHIPWRECK

THEA STILTON AND THE SECRET CITY

**THEA STILTON AND THE
MYSTERY IN PARIS**

**THEA STILTON AND THE CHERRY
BLOSSOM ADVENTURE**

**THEA STILTON AND THE
STAR CASTAWAYS**

**THEA STILTON: BIG TROUBLE
IN THE BIG APPLE**

**THEA STILTON AND THE
ICE TREASURE**

**THEA STILTON AND THE
SECRET OF THE OLD CASTLE**

1. Mountains of the Mangy Yeti
2. Cacklefur Castle
3. Angry Walnut Tree
4. Rattenbaum Mansion
5. Rancidrat River
6. Bridge of Shaky Steps
7. Squeakspeare Mansion
8. Slimy Swamp
9. Ogre Highway
10. Gloomeria
11. Shivery Arts Academy
12. Horrorwood Studios

CACKLEFUR CASTLE

1. Oozing moat

2. Drawbridge

3. Grand entrance

4. Moldy basement

5. Patio, with a view of the moat

6. Dusty library

7. Room for unwanted guests

8. Mummy room

9. Watchtower

10. Creaking staircase

11. Banquet room

12. Garage (for antique hearses)

13. Bewitched tower

14. Garden of carnivorous plants

15. Stinky kitchen

16. Crocodile pool and piranha tank

17. Creepella's room

18. Tower of musky tarantulas

19. Bitewing's tower (with antique contraptions)

DEAR MOUSE FRIENDS, GOOD-BYE UNTIL THE NEXT BOOK!